THE BEST JOKES FOR

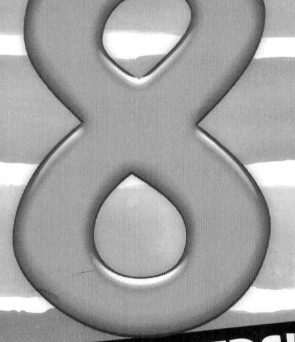

8

YEAR OLD KIDS!

OVER 250 FUNNY

With over 250 really funny,
hilarious Jokes,
The Best Jokes For 8 Year Old Kids!
promises hours of fun for
the whole family!

Includes brand new, original and
classic Jokes that will have the kids
(and adults!) in fits of laughter
in no time!

These jokes are so funny it's going
to be hard not to laugh!
Just wait until you hear the
giggles and laughter!

Books by Freddy Frost

The Best Jokes For 6 Year Old Kids
The Best Jokes For 7 Year Old Kids
The Best Jokes For 8 Year Old Kids
The Best Jokes For 9 Year Old Kids
The Best Jokes For 10 Year Old Kids
The Best Jokes For 11 Year Old Kids
The Best Jokes For 12 Year Old Kids

To see all the latest books by Freddy Frost just go to
FreddyFrost.com

Contents

Funny Q & A Jokes!

What do you get if you cross
an alligator with a camera?
A snapshot!

Which side of a chicken has
the most feathers?
The outside!

Why did the monkey have a day off?
Work was driving him bananas!

Why didn't the skeleton
play church music?
He had no organs!

Where did the butcher go
on Saturday night?
The Meatball!

Which monster loves
April Fools Day?
Prankenstein!

How do birds learn to fly for the very first time?
They wing it!

Why did the ghost catch a cold?
He got chilled to the bone!

What did the hedgehog say to the cactus?
Hi dad!

What do you call a skeleton
that sleeps in?
Lazy Bones!

Why was the spider hanging out
on the computer?
He was making a website!

Why was the deer at the dentist?
He had buck teeth!

What starts with gas but only
has 3 letters?
A car!

Where did the shark post
his photos?
Finstagram!

If you put a snake and a pie into a
magician's hat, what would you have?
A pie-thon!

How do electric eels taste?

Shocking!

What did the jar of marmalade wear to bed?

Jammies!

Why did the man have so much facial hair?

It seemed to just grow on him!

Why was the fullback scared to go on the plane?
In case the coach put him on the wing!

Why was the Mexican restaurant so popular?
It was the taco the town!

What did Adam say on the night before Christmas?
It's Christmas, Eve!

What do toads play after school?
Leapfrog!

Why did the boy take his
ruler to bed?
To see how long he slept!

What did the astronaut drink
on his break?
A nice cup of gravi-tea!

What do you call an alligator
who eats Mars Bars?
A chocho-dile!

What do you call a pig that was
caught speeding?
A road hog!

Why don't pigs play football?
They hog the ball!

Why did the whale blush?
She saw the ocean's bottom!

What do you have if 2 snakes
are on your car window?
Window Vipers!

What can you use to open
the great lakes?
The Florida Keys!

What do you call a polar bear
in the desert?

Lost!

How did the wrinkled dress feel?

De-pressed!

Why did the raspberry call 911?

She was in a jam!

Why is a guitar opposite to a fish?
**A guitar can be tuned but
you can't tuna fish!**

What do you call 28 rabbits walking
in a row backwards?
A receding hareline!

Why did the orange fail her
math test?
She couldn't concentrate!

What did one angel say to the other angel?

Halo!

What do ghosts eat for lunch?

Spook-getthi!

What do you get if you cross a duck with a rooster?

A bird that wakes you up at the quack of dawn!

Funnier Knock Knock Jokes!

Knock knock.

Who's there?

Don.

Don who?

Don ya want to open the door before I freeze to death!

Knock knock.

Who's there?

Kenya.

Kenya who?

Kenya guess who is coming to my place for dinner?
Uncle Bob!

Knock knock.

Who's there?

Needle.

Needle who?

Needle little help with the shopping! I bought too much!

Knock knock.

Who's there?

Imma.

Imma who?

Imma getting a bit wet out here in the rain! Please let me in!

Knock knock.

Who's there?

Avenue.

Avenue who?

Avenue fixed the doorbell yet? It's been 2 years!

Knock knock.

Who's there?

Chicken.

Chicken who?

Better Chicken the oven! Something is burning!

Knock knock.

Who's there?

Butternut.

Butternut who?

Butternut be late!
Let's go right now!

Knock knock.

Who's there?

Java.

Java who?

Java cup of sugar for my mom?
We ran out!

Knock knock.

Who's there?

Sienna.

Sienna who?

Sienna good movies lately?

Knock knock.

Who's there?

Pudding.

Pudding who?

I'm pudding on my best dress for dinner! Do you like it?

Knock knock.

Who's there?

Avon.

Avon who?

Avon you to open ze door!

Knock knock.

Who's there?

Lena.

Lena who?

Lena bit closer and I'll tell you all about it!

Knock knock.

Who's there?

Noise.

Noise who?

Noise to see you again after all this time! How are the kids?

Knock knock.

Who's there?

Nobel.

Nobel who?

Nobel so I knocked!

Knock knock.

Who's there?

Robin.

Robin who?

**He's Robin your house!
Call the Police!**

Knock knock.

Who's there?

Phone.

Phone who?

**Phone-ly I had known you
were home I would have
knocked earlier!**

Knock knock.

Who's there?

Saul.

Saul who?

Saul there is! There's none left! Sorry!

Knock knock.

Who's there?

Abel.

Abel who?

Abel would mean I don't have to knock!

Knock knock.

Who's there?

Rabbit.

Rabbit who?

**Rabbit up neatly please.
It's a present!**

Knock knock.

Who's there?

Ooze.

Ooze who?

**Ooze in charge here
my good sir?**

Knock knock.

Who's there?

Some Bunny.

Some Bunny who?

**Some Bunny has eaten
my lunch!
Nooooo!**

Knock knock.

Who's there?

Police.

Police who?

**Police hurry up and open
this door!
I have knocked 8 times!**

Knock knock.

Who's there?

Mikey.

Mikey who?

Mikey doesn't fit!
Why did you change the lock?

Knock knock.

Who's there?

Tank.

Tank who?

Tank goodness you finally
answered the door!

Knock knock.

Who's there?

Jim.

Jim who?

**Jim mind if I stay for a while?
I got locked out of
my own house!**

Knock knock.

Who's there?

Ogre.

Ogre who?

**Can you come Ogre for
dinner tonight?
We're having candy on toast!**

Laugh Out Loud Q & A Jokes!

What do you call a nose with no body, no head or eyes - just a nose?
Nobody nose!

What did the cannon name his son?
A son of a gun!

Where do rabbits go after they get married?
On their Bunnymoon!

What happened to the fish
who played tennis?

He got caught in the net!

Why can cows speak to ghosts?

They are on the udder side!

What do you get if you cross a
rooster with a poodle?

A CockaPoodleDoo!

What do you call a frog sitting
on a chair?
A toadstool!

What do you call a dog with
a sore throat?
A husky!

Why did the mushroom take
dance lessons?
He was a fungi (fun guy)!

Why did he have to quit dance lessons?
There wasn't mush room!

What do you call a vampire
Santa Claus?
Sackula!

What do cows look at in the museum?
The Mooona Lisa!

Why did the swimmer stop swimming?
The sea weed!

What is the name of the cat that lives at the hospital?
First aid kit!

Why did the butterfly leave the dance?
It was a moth ball!

What do nuts say if they catch a cold?
Cashew!

What is Santa's dog called?

Santa Paws!

Why did the robber duck?

The policeman threw the book at him!

Why are fish good in a choir?

They practice their scales!

What do you use to wrap a cloud?
A rainbow!

What did the thief get after he
stole a calendar?
12 months!

Why did the witch itch?
She lost her W!

What was the Monster's favorite type of cheese?
Monsterella!

Why couldn't the astronaut go to the moon?
It was full!

What type of markets do dogs hate?
Flea markets!

What did one plate say to the other plate?

Dinner's on me!

What sport does Dracula play?

Bat-minton!

Where did the pencil go for his vacation?

Pencil Vania!

What do you have if an elephant
sits on your friend?
A flat mate!

What do you call a pig that
can do kung fu?
A pork chop!

What is the worst day to get eaten
by a tiger?
Chewsday!

What happens if you feed
gun powder to chickens?

Egg-splosions!

Why did the boy pour hot water
down a rabbit hole?

**He wanted some hot
cross bunnies!**

Why did the girl bring a
ladder to music class?

To help her sing the high notes!

How do you stop a bull from charging?
Take away its credit card!

Why did the artist become a nurse?
So she could draw blood!

If a boomerang doesn't come back, what is it?
A stick!

What is the wettest animal?
A rain-deer!

Why did the tissue dance
all night long?
It was full of boogey!

What do you call a fairy who hasn't
had a shower for 3 weeks?
Stinker Bell!

Crazy Knock Knock Jokes!

Knock knock.

Who's there?

Mushroom.

Mushroom who?

Do you have mushroom left in the car? I have 4 suitcases!

Knock knock.

Who's there?

Sawyer.

Sawyer who?

Sawyer lights on so I thought I would knock!

Knock knock.

Who's there?

Iona.

Iona who?

**Iona brand new car!
Come and see!**

Knock knock.

Who's there?

Hada.

Hada who?

**Hada great weekend!
How about you?**

Knock knock.

Who's there?

Cain.

Cain who?

**Cain you give me a lift to school?
I'm really late!**

Knock knock.

Who's there?

Harmony.

Harmony who?

**Harmony times do I
have to knock?
Please answer the door!**

Knock knock.

Who's there?

Jaws.

Jaws who?

Jaws truly! Surprise!

Knock knock.

Who's there?

Phillip.

Phillip who?

**Phillip your pool so
we can swim!
Yayyy!**

Knock knock.

Who's there?

Tweet.

Tweet who?

**Would you like tweet an apple?
They are really tasty!**

Knock knock.

Who's there?

Leon.

Leon who?

**You can Leon me if your
leg is still sore!**

Knock knock.

Who's there?

Dishes.

Dishes who?

**Dishes me, remember?
We met last week!**

Knock knock.

Who's there?

Red.

Red who?

**Red quite a few jokes today
so let's read a few more!**

Knock knock.

Who's there?

CD.

Cd who?

**CD big clouds?
It's gonna rain!**

Knock knock.

Who's there?

Amos.

Amos who?

**Amos say you look great
in that suit.
Where did you get it?**

Knock knock.

Who's there?

Emerson.

Emerson who?

**Emerson nice socks you have on.
Did you get them at Kmart?**

Knock knock.

Who's there?

Alma.

Alma who?

**Alma candy has gone!
Nooooo!**

Knock knock.

Who's there?

Fanny.

Fanny who?

Fanny body knocks just pretend you're not home!

Knock knock.

Who's there?

Candice.

Candice who?

Candice bell actually ring because I have pressed it 12 times!

Knock knock.

Who's there?

Figs.

Figs who?

**Figs the doorbell please.
All this knocking hurts my hand!**

Knock knock.

Who's there?

House.

House who?

**House it going my
dearest friend?**

Knock knock.

Who's there?

Onya.

Onya who?

**Onya marks! Get set!
Go!**

Knock knock.

Who's there?

Argo.

Argo who?

**Argo to school in the morning,
but first I need some sleep!**

Knock knock.

Who's there?

Sir.

Sir who?

Sir prise!
I bet you weren't expecting me,
were you?

Knock knock.

Who's there?

Noah.

Noah who?

Noah good place for lunch?
How about pizza?

Knock knock.

Who's there?

Amin.

Amin who?

Amin already so don't worry about the door!

Knock knock.

Who's there?

Jess.

Jess who?

Jess let me in please! I need to pee!

Ridiculous Q & A Jokes!

What kind of books do skunks read?
Best Smellers!

How do koalas fight?
With their bear hands!

Why did the bowling pins fall over?
They were on strike!

What do you call a mountain climber?
Cliff!

What happens when 2 silkworms
have a race?
It ends in a tie!

Why didn't the lady trust the artist?
He seemed a bit sketchy!

Why didn't the girl want to
kiss the vampire?
It's such a pain in the neck!

What did the doctor say to the
patient who only had one tooth?
Just grin and bare it!

What was the apple doing at
the gym?
Working on his core!

What do you call a boy who hits
a baseball over the fence?
Homer!

What do Cannibals call athletes?
Fast Food!

What has four wheels, weighs 10 tons
and flies?
A garbage truck!

What do you call a crazy loaf of bread.
A weir-dough!

What do you call a hippo with
a messy room?
A Hippopota Mess!

What is a dinosaur's favorite car?
A Rexus!

How did the angel light
her camp fire?
**She used a match made
in heaven!**

What was the snake's favorite
subject at snake school?
Hiss-story!

Which part of the eye always
does the most work?
The pupil!

Why are poodles so good to
be around?

They are very paws-itive!

What's the cheapest way to
buy an elephant?

At a jumbo sale!

Why did the crocodile buy a GPS?

To be a navi-Gator!

What do you call a man lifting
a car with his hands?

Jack!

What did the ghost cow say?

MooooOOOOOooooOOOOoooo!

What does every winner lose
in a race?

Their breath!

Why do French people eat snails?
They don't like fast food!

Why did the teacher go to the pool?
To test the water!

Why was the chicken student sad?
She failed her eggs-ams!

Where is Dracula's office?
The Vampire State Building!

What do puppies eat at the movies?
Pupcorn!

What do you give a lemon that
has hurt itself?
Lemon-ade!

What did the big steak say to
the little steak?

So! We meat again!

Why was the computer teacher scared?

She saw a mouse!

What should you give a pig who
has a rash?

Some oinkment!

Why was the watch really bored?
**He had too much time
on his hands!**

Why did the restaurant on
the moon close?
It had no atmosphere!

Why are skeletons always so calm?
Nothing gets under their skin!

Why did the farmer drive a
steam roller through his field?
**He wanted to grow
mashed potatoes!**

Why did the cat swim?
She was a platy-puss!

Why did the almond jump
up and down?
It was going nuts!

Silly Knock Knock Jokes!

Knock knock.

Who's there?

Ada.

Ada who?

Ada sandwich for my lunch and it was yummy!

Knock knock.

Who's there?

Alpaca.

Alpaca who?

Alpaca the suitcase, you pack a the trunk!

Knock knock.

Who's there?

Abby.

Abby who?

Abby stung me on my foot. OWWWWWWWW!!

Knock knock.

Who's there?

Candy.

Candy who?

Candy owner of the dog come outside? It won't stop barking!

Knock knock.

Who's there?

Cook.

Cook who?

Are you a cuckoo clock?

Knock knock.

Who's there?

Justin.

Justin who?

Justin case you didn't know, it's going to rain in a minute!

Knock knock.

Who's there?

Ari.

Ari who?

**Ari there yet?
It's been 5 hours!**

Knock knock.

Who's there?

Freddy.

Freddy who?

**Freddy set, go!
I'll race you to the letterbox!**

Knock knock.

Who's there?

Barbie.

Barbie who?

Barbie Q for dinner!
Yummy!

Knock knock.

Who's there?

Kent.

Kent who?

Kent you see I want to come in!
I've been waiting for 3 hours!

Knock knock.

Who's there?

Ray.

Ray who?

Ray member when we first met?
Love at first sight!

Knock knock.

Who's there?

Roach.

Roach who?

Roach you 3 letters but
you never replied!

Knock knock.

Who's there?

Kanye.

Kanye who?

Kanye give me a hand with this parcel? It's really heavy!

Knock knock.

Who's there?

Cheese.

Cheese who?

Cheese a very good singer. Want to see her new band?

Knock knock.

Who's there?

Emma.

Emma who?

Emma very hungry!
How about candy for lunch?

Knock knock.

Who's there?

Amy.

Amy who?

Amy fraid I can't remember!
What was the question again?

Knock knock.

Who's there?

Sid.

Sid who?

Sid you would be ready by now!
Why are you late?

Knock knock.

Who's there?

Adair.

Adair who?

Adair when I was younger
but now I'm bald!

Knock knock.

Who's there?

Razor.

Razor who?

Razor hands in the air like you just don't care!

Knock knock.

Who's there?

Tick.

Tick who?

Tick 'em up! I'm a wobber!

Knock knock.

Who's there?

Pop.

Pop who?

**Pop on over to my place.
We're having ice cream!**

Knock knock.

Who's there?

Meg.

Meg who?

Meg up your mind and let me in!

Knock knock.

Who's there?

Oliver.

Oliver who?

Oliver other kids are busy so can you help me do my chores?

Knock knock.

Who's there?

Doughnut.

Doughnut who?

I Doughnut know but I will find out!

Knock knock.

Who's there?

Troy.

Troy who?

Troy to be quicker next time please!

Knock knock.

Who's there?

Turnip.

Turnip who?

Turnip the music! Let's party!

Bonus
Q & A Jokes!

What do you call a boy on
your doorstep?
Matt!

What do you call a dinosaur
with only one eye?
A Do-You-Think-They-Saurus!

Which cat works at the hospital?
The first aid kit!

Why wasn't the scarecrow
very hungry?
He was already stuffed!

What kind of sandwich did the
shark order for his lunch?
Peanut butter and jellyfish!

Why did the pilot paint flowers
on his jet?
It was too plane!

What do you call a naked man?
Seymour!

Which nails do carpenters try
not to hit?
Fingernails!

How can you make friends
with a squirrel?
**Climb up a tree and act
like a nut!**

Why did the chicken quit laying eggs?
She was too eggs-hausted!

What was the fake noodle's
Secret Agent name?
The Impasta!

What was the fly doing in
the bowl of soup?
Backstroke!

Why do hard boiled eggs always win at cards?

They are hard to beat!

Why did the frog say Mooooo?

He was learning another language!

Why did the thermometer go to college?

To get more degrees!

What do cats eat for desert?
Mice cream!

What do you call a lady
climbing a wall?
Ivy!

What did the hamburger name
his daughter?
Patty!

Why are dalmatians no
good at hiding?

They are easy to spot!

What did the toilet roll say
to the toilet?

You're looking a bit flushed!

What washes up on the smallest
beach in the world?

Microwaves!

How do divers sleep under the sea?
They use a snore-kel!

Which dessert is no fun to eat?
Apple Grumble!

Why did the teacher wear
dark sunglasses?
Her students were too bright!

How did the slug do in his math test?
He snailed it!

What stays in the corner and
then travels all over the country?
A stamp!

What happens if a dog eats
way too much garlic?
His bark is worse than his bite!

What do you call a potato that
joined the monastery?

A chip monk!

What is the wind's favorite color?

Blew!

What do you call a woman with
a wooden leg?

Peg!

Which bird owns a bank?
The ost-rich!

What did the boxer drink just
before the big fight?
Fruit punch!

What did the panda say on
Halloween night?
Bam-BOOO!

What is the proper name for a camel with 3 humps?

Humphrey!

Which cell phones taste yummy?

Blackberries!

What was written on the robot's gravestone?

Rust in Peace!

Why did the driver put vegetables
in his radiator?
To soup up the engine!

What did the pencil say to the pen?
Write on brother!

How did the first flying monkey
get to work?
In her hot air baboon!

Bonus
Knock Knock Jokes!

Knock knock.

Who's there?

Father.

Father who?

Father last time please open the door before I freeze!

Knock knock.

Who's there?

Freeze.

Freeze who?

Freeze a jolly good fellowwww!

Knock knock.

Who's there?

Dingo.

Dingo who?

Dingo anywhere yesterday! How about you?

Knock knock.

Who's there?

Athena.

Athena who?

Athena shooting star last night so I made a wish!

Knock knock.

Who's there?

Harry.

Harry who?

**Harry up!
It's so cold a penguin
would freeze!**

Knock knock.

Who's there?

Riot.

Riot who?

I'm Riot on time so let's go!

Knock knock.

Who's there?

Gino.

Gino who?

Gino me really well so open the door!

Knock knock.

Who's there?

Bean.

Bean who?

Bean waiting here for ages! Why are you always so late?

Knock knock.

Who's there?

Cannelloni.

Cannelloni who?

Cannelloni 5 bucks until next week?

Knock knock.

Who's there?

Locky.

Locky who?

Locky I caught you before you went out!

Knock knock.

Who's there?

Dozen.

Dozen who?

Dozen all this knocking get a bit annoying?
Ha Ha!!

Knock knock.

Who's there?

Owl.

Owl who?

Owl be sure to use the doorbell tomorrow!

Knock knock.

Who's there?

Snow.

Snow who?

Snow business like show business!

Knock knock.

Who's there?

Beth.

Beth who?

Beth friends stick together so let's go!

Knock knock.

Who's there?

Thor.

Thor who?

My arm is Thor from carrying this heavy bag! Owwww!

Knock knock.

Who's there?

Diet.

Diet who?

You can change your hair color if you diet!

Knock knock.

Who's there?

Ferdie.

Ferdie who?

Ferdie last time please open up!

Knock knock.

Who's there?

Myth.

Myth who?

I myth you tho much when I don't thee you!

Knock knock.

Who's there?

Cattle.

Cattle who?

Cattle purr if you pat it!

Knock knock.

Who's there?

Hank.

Hank who?

You are so welcome sir!

Knock knock.

Who's there?

Amish.

Amish who?

You're not a shoe, you're a person!

Knock knock.

Who's there?

Duncan.

Duncan who?

Duncan doughnuts go really well with ice cream!

Knock knock.

Who's there?

Poor me.

Poor me who?

Poor me a glass of water! I'm really thirsty!

Knock knock.

Who's there?

Sonia.

Sonia who?

Sonia shoe! It's quite stinky! Ewwwwww!

Thank you!

.... so much for reading our book.

We hope you had lots of laughs and enjoyed these funny jokes.

We would appreciate it so much if you could leave us a review on Amazon. Reviews make a big difference and we appreciate your support. Thank you!

Our Joke Books are available as a series for all ages from 6-12.

To see our range of books or leave a review anytime please go to
FreddyFrost.com.

Thanks again!

Freddy Frost

Made in the USA
San Bernardino, CA
26 November 2019

60453107R00062